To my friend Marcia

Printed in Singapore
Reinforced binding

First Edition, April 2007
10 9 8 7
F850-6835-5-15041

Library of Congress Cataloging-in-Publication Data
Willems, Mo.
My friend is sad/by Mo Willems
p. cm.—(An Elephant and Piggie book)
Summary: When Gerald the Elephant is sad, Piggie is determined to cheer him up, but
finds after many tries that it only takes the simplest thing to change Gerald's mood.
ISBN-10: 1-4231-0297-5 (alk. paper)
ISBN-13: 978-1-4231-0297-7
[1. Pigs—Fiction. 2. Elephants—Fiction. 3. Emotions—Fiction. 4. Friendship—Fiction.]
I. Title
PZ7.W6553My 2007
[E]—dc22
2006049582

Visit www.hyperionbooksforchildren.com and www.pigeonpresents.com

My Friend Is Sad

By Mo Willems

An ELEPHANT & PIGGIE Book
Hyperion Books for Children/*New York*

9

A cowboy!

Clowns are funny.
But he is still sad.

How can anyone be sad around a robot!?

Ohhh . . .

Gerald.

Piggie!

I am sorry. I wanted
to make you happy.
But you are still sad.

29

But I was so sad, Piggie. So very SAD!

But you love cowboys!

Then I saw a clown!

THERE
WAS
MORE!

I saw a ROBOT!

47

And my best friend
was not there
to see it with me.

I am here NOW!

My friend is here now!

I need my friends.

You need new glasses....

Elephant and Piggie have more funny adventures in: